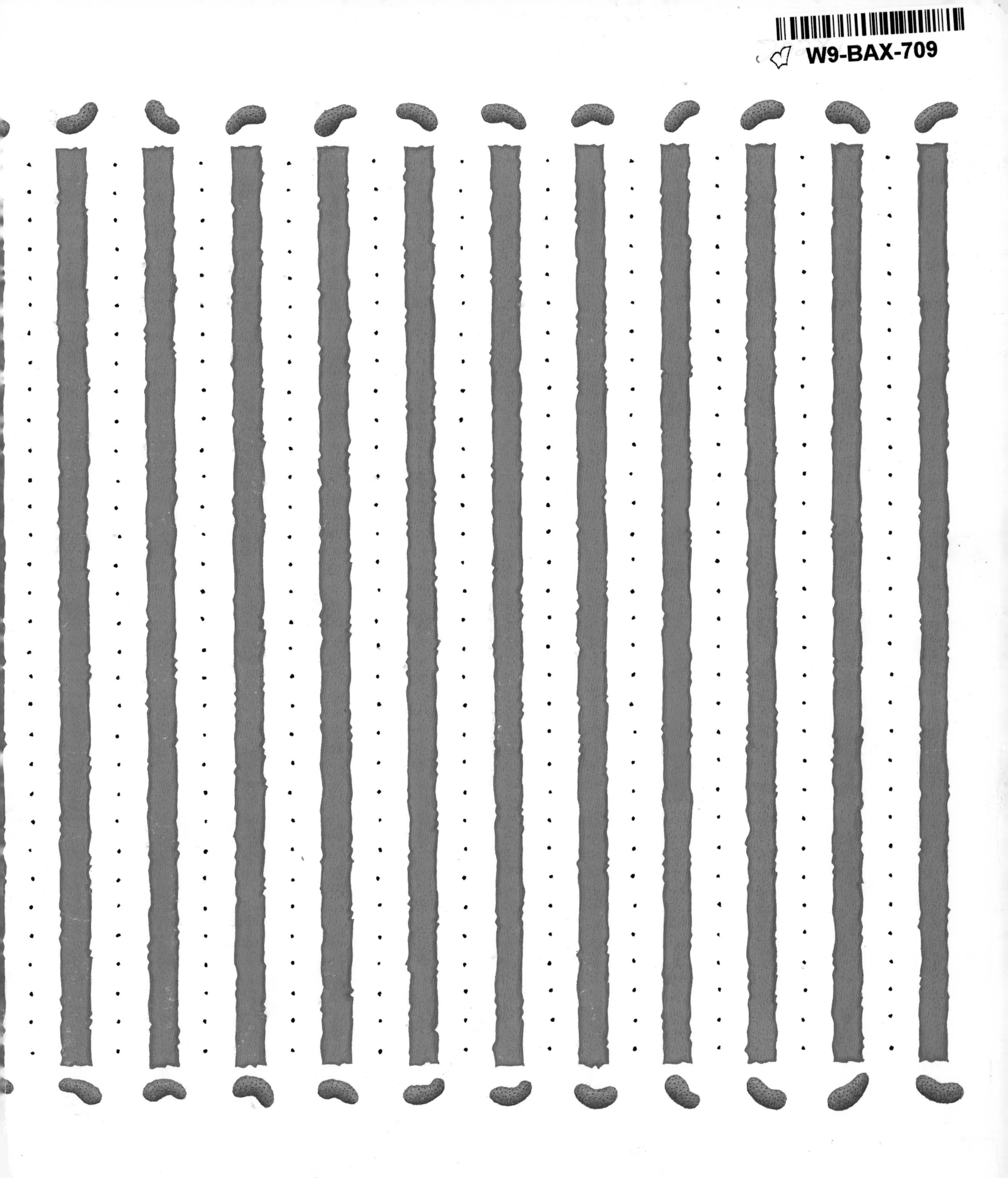

Picky Mrs. Pickle

Christine M. Schneider

Walker and Company
New York

First published in the United States of America in 1999 by Walker Publishing Company, Inc.

Published simultaneously in Canada by Fitzhenry and Whiteside, Markham, Ontario L3R 4T8

Library of Congress Cataloging-in-Publication Data
Schneider, Christine M.
Picky Mrs. Pickle/Christine M. Schneider.
p. cm.
Summary: After years of wearing only green clothes and eating only pickle foods, picky Mrs. Pickle learns that trying something new can be fun.
ISBN 0-8027-8702-9 (hc.). —ISBN 0-8027-8703-7 (reinforced)
[1. Self-perception Fiction. 2. Stories in rhyme.] I. Title.
PZ8.3.S365Pi 1999
[E]—dc21 99-26025
CIP

Book design by Christine M. Schneider and Sophie Ye Chin

Printed in Hong Kong

4 6 8 10 9 7 5 3

For Mom, who makes the most delicious dill pickles in the world.

Picky Mrs. Pickle won't try anything at all.
Nothing but green dresses fill her closet in the hall.

PICKLES

She has her favorite color
and her favorite pickle pie.

She has a favorite perfume too,
no others will she buy.

She won’t try a new hairdo, and she won’t try a new hat.

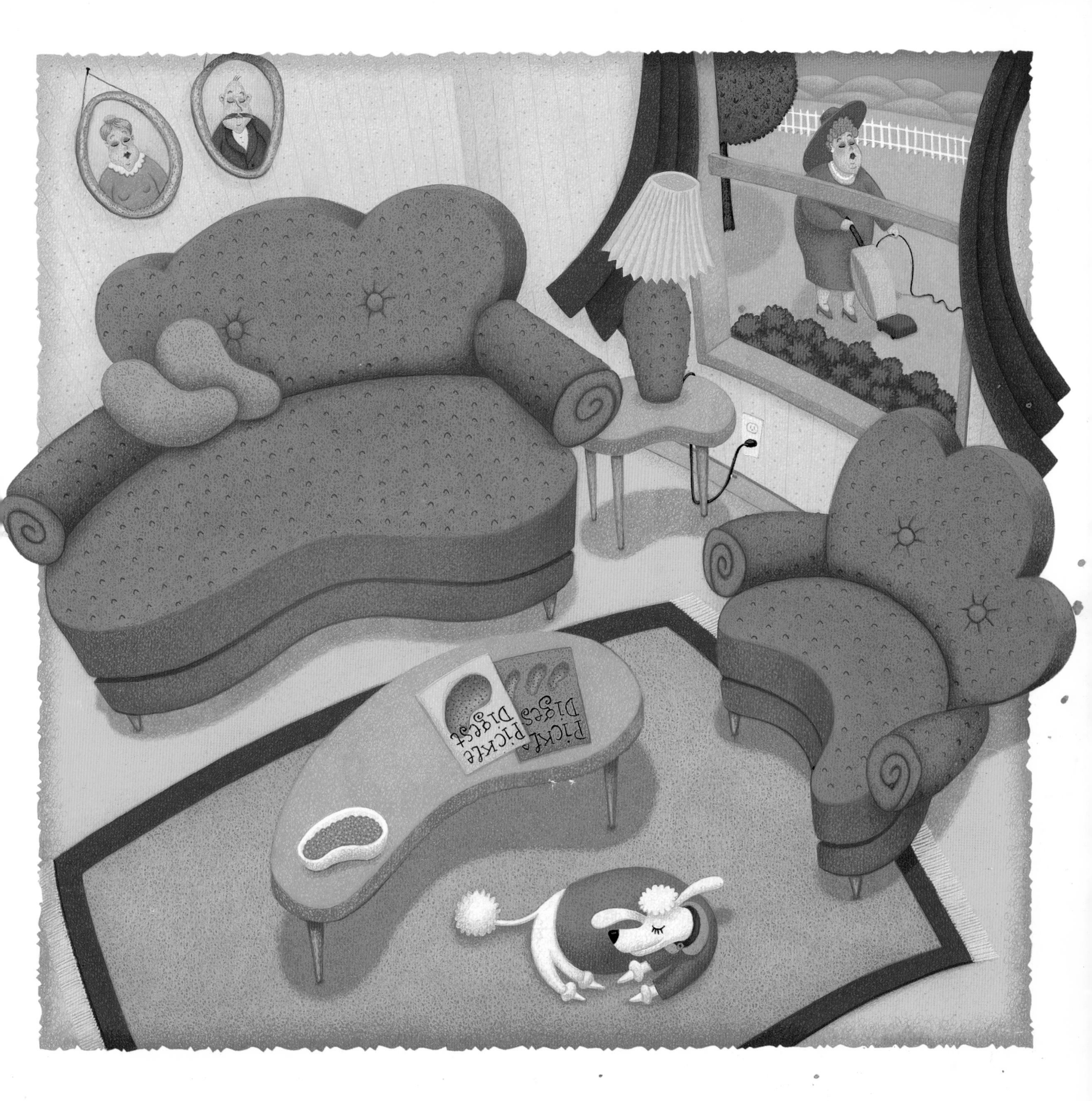

She likes the way her house looks with the green lawn nice and flat.

New exhibit
GNU exhibit

When picky Mrs. Pickle
makes a visit to the zoo,

she won't go look at anything
except the hairy gnu.

She buys a lot of pretty shoes; in fact, she can't keep track.
There's minty green and grassy green, but never red or black.

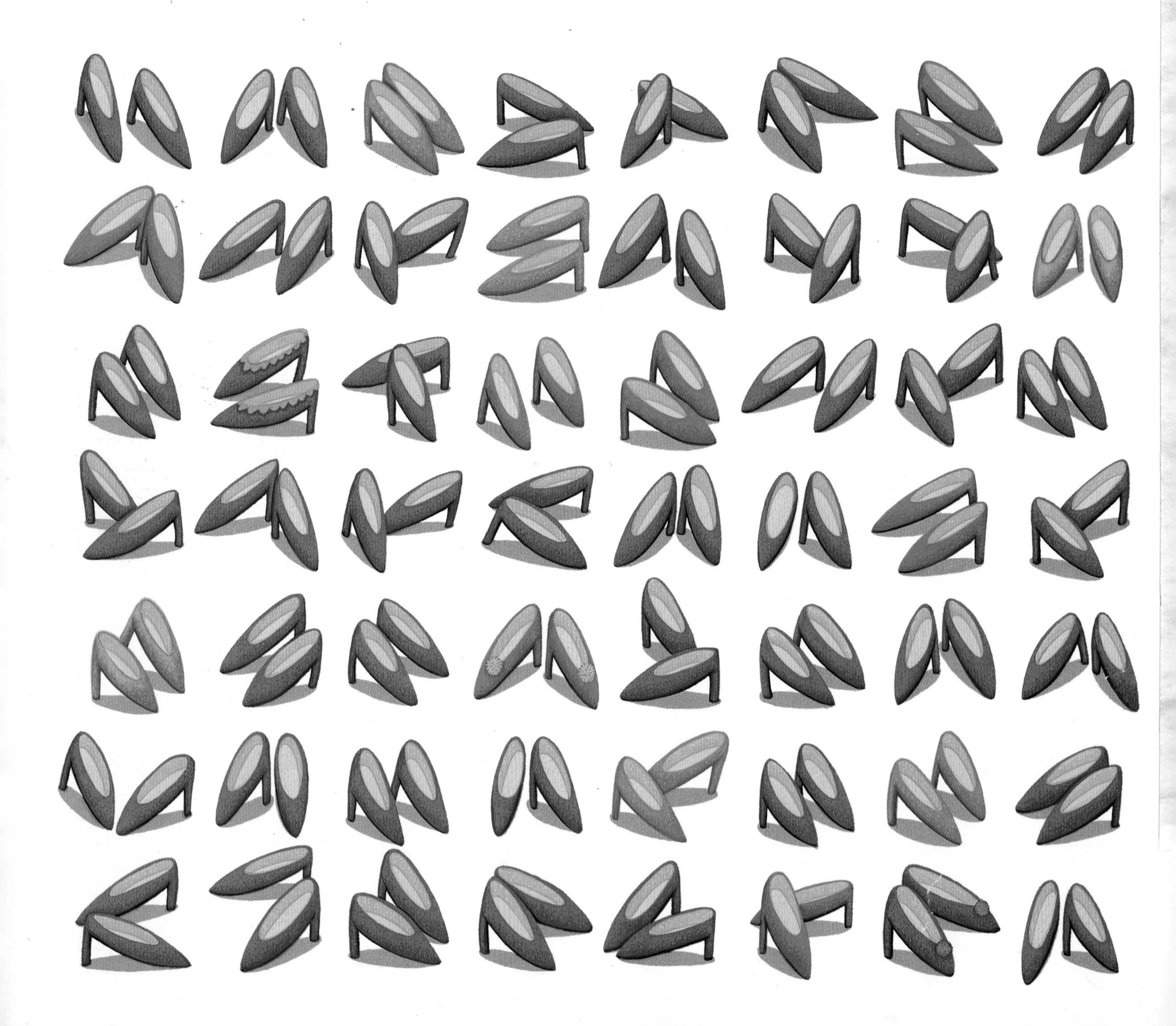

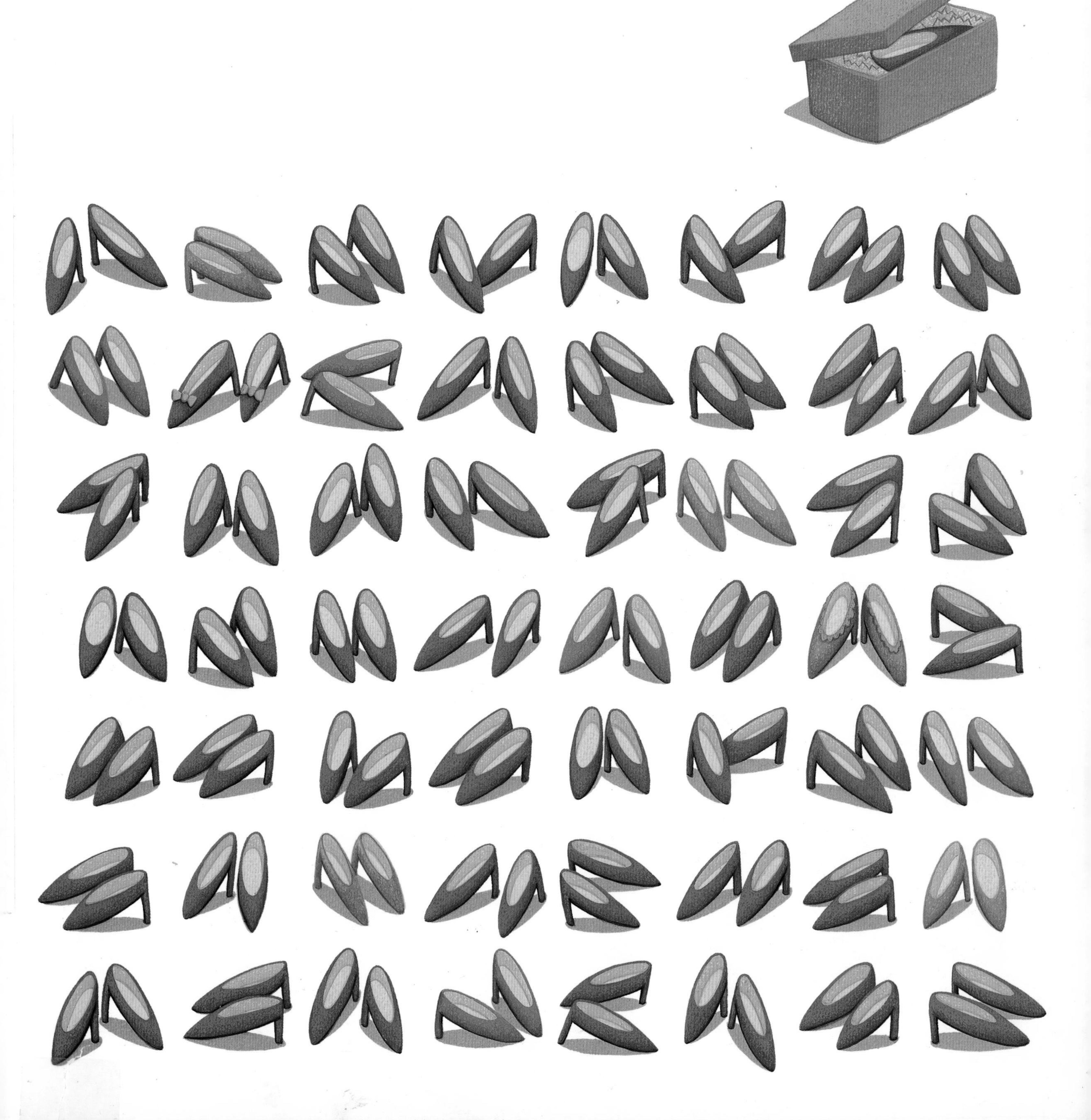

Picky Mrs. Pickle won't make any brand new friends.
"It's far too hard! It's too much work!" she's happy to pretend.

WIGS & TOUPEES
Ritzy Mitzi's
GOURMET
PICKLE
Palace
GROCERY
NOGGIN
Boutique

"I like the things I like," she says. "I'm very sure of that."

"I needn't ever change because I'm happy where I'm at."

Even her own family
knows it's useless
to point out

that pickles and
green shoes are not
what life is all about.

Little Sophie Claire,
however, always
speaks her mind.

She's Mrs. Pickle's
youngest niece,
and she's
one of a kind.

Every Sunday afternoon
the two walk hand in hand,

down the road and up one block
to Igor's ice cream stand.

Every week they disagree
when Sophie begs her aunt

to try a different flavor
—like tomato or eggplant.

IGOR'S
ce cream

"How do you know if you won't try
a new kind of ice cream

that you wouldn't like it better
than you ever even dreamed?"

She tells her aunt her attitude
is silly and unfair—

"I think you won't try something new
because you're just plain scared."

This week was not
a different one, they
argued just the same,

but stubborn Sophie
stood her ground and
once again took aim.

"If you just try a
tiny bite, I'll make
a deal with you.

I'll walk your dog for
one whole year and
polish all your shoes."

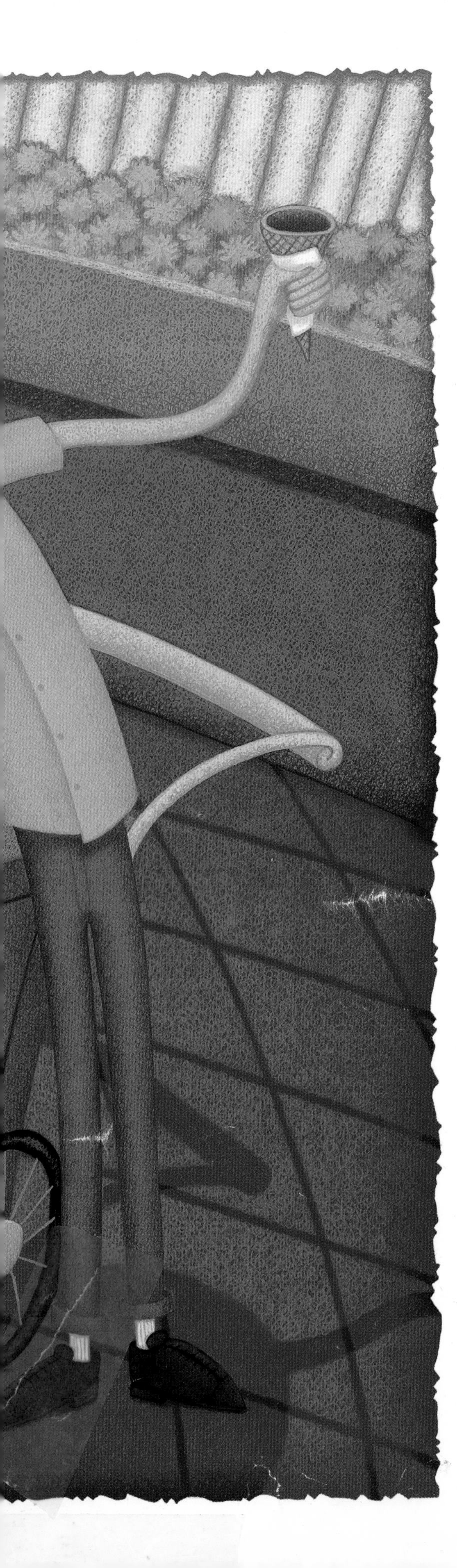

Picky Mrs. Pickle couldn't
pass up such a trade.

She finally got her nerve up
and she thought, "I'm not afraid!"

"A scoop of eggplant ripple, please?"
she swallowed hard and asked.

She closed her eyes, she licked a lick,
and then she gasped a gasp.

Daily Post
PICKLE
EATS
EGGPLANT

Café

Surprise, surprise! You'll never guess! She liked it even more than any ice cream, cake, or pie she'd ever had before!

"My, this is strange! How could this be? I thought it would taste bad! I thought I only liked the things that I'd already had."

"I'll learn to dance! I'll learn to paint!
I'll learn how to speak French!

I have a thirst to try new things
that never can be quenched!"

"New things to try, new friends to make,
no wonder I was bored!"

Now picky Mrs. Pickle
isn't picky anymore!

S.S. Eggplant

Learn to dance the
Rutabaga
Rhumba!
3
5
4
1
2
6

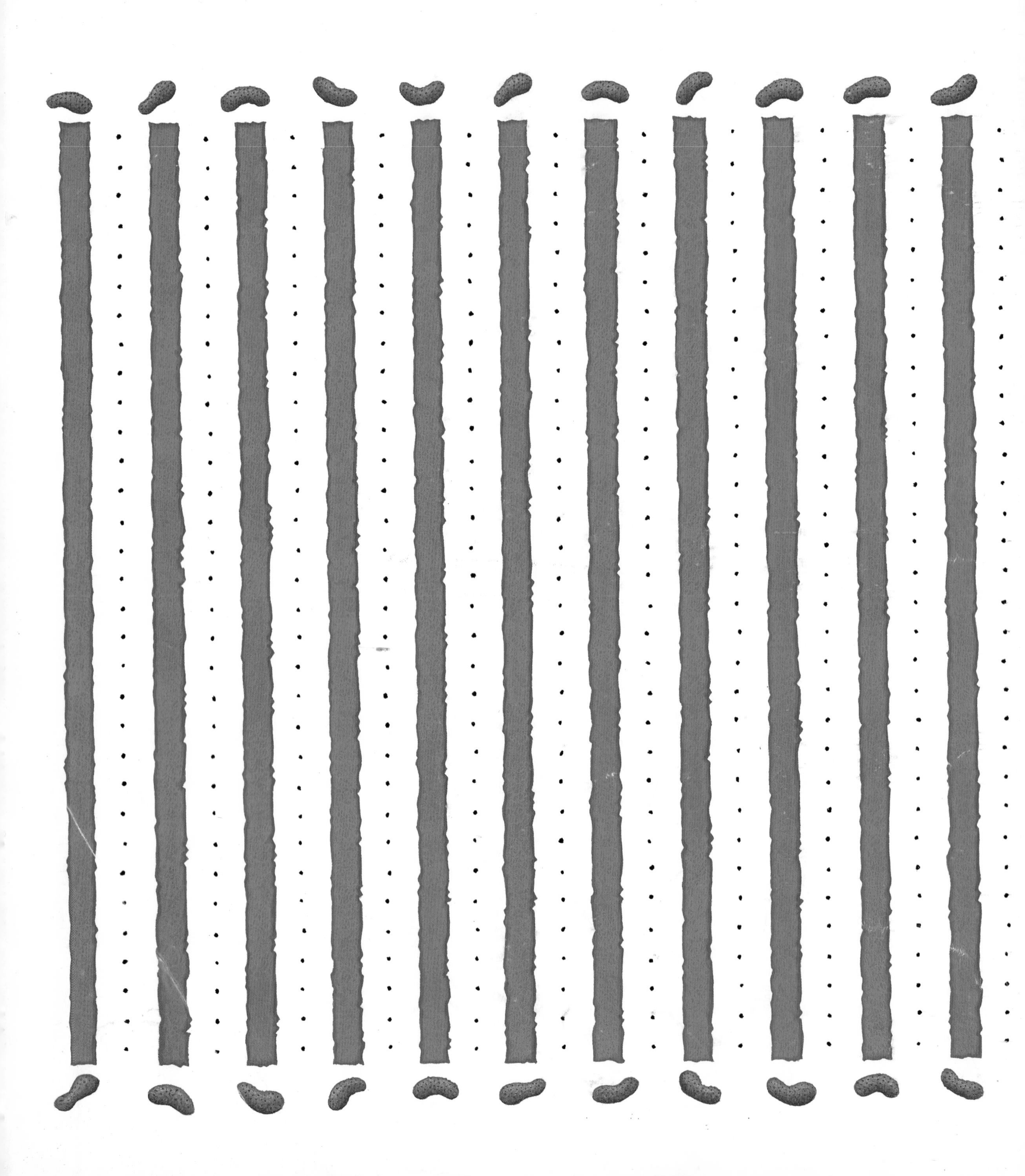